CHI 2/07

ALLEN COUNTY PUBLIC LIBRARY

FRIENDS
OF ACPL

3 1833 05143 6803

SO-BND-295

Moving Machines

Patty Whitehouse

Rourke

Publishing LLC

Vero Beach, Florida 32964

Allen County Public Library

© 2007 Rourke Publishing LLC

All rights reserved. No part of this book may be reproduced or utilized in any form or by any means, electronic or mechanical including photocopying, recording, or by any information storage and retrieval system without permission in writing from the publisher.

www.rourkepublishing.com

PHOTO CREDITS: © David and Patricia Armentrout: pages 13, 19, 20, 22; © Craig Lopetz: pages 5, 14, 17, 18; © PIR: pages 6, 7, 8, 10, 11; © constructionphotographs.com: pages 9, 12, 15, 16, 21; © Steven Robertson: page 4

Editor: Robert Stengard-Olliges

Cover and interior design by Nicola Stratford

Library of Congress Cataloging-in-Publication Data

Whitehouse, Patricia, 1958-
 Moving machines / Patty Whitehouse.
     p. cm. -- (Construction forces)
 Includes index.
 ISBN 1-60044-192-0 (hardcover)
 ISBN 1-59515-549-X (softcover)
 1. Hoisting machinery--Juvenile literature. 2. Materials
handling--Juvenile literature. 3. Motion--Juvenile literature. 4. Building
sites--Juvenile literature. I. Title. II. Series: Whitehouse, Patricia,
1958- Construction forces.
 TJ1350.W48 2007
 621.8'6--dc22
                                        2006008861

Printed in the USA

CG/CG

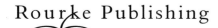

Rourke Publishing

www.rourkepublishing.com – sales@rourkepublishing.com
Post Office Box 3328, Vero Beach, FL 32964
1-800-394-7055

Table of Contents

Construction Site Machines

This is a **construction site**. There are many **machines** here.

Some machines move. Machines that move can build or tear down.

Machines for Moving

Ramp

The ramp and the shovel are machines, too. They are called simple machines.

Shovel

They do not have parts that move. But they make moving things easier. This shovel moves dirt.

Moving on a Ramp

A **wheelbarrow** is moving up the ramp. The ramp is a machine that makes moving up or down easier.

A cement chute is a ramp, too. It moves cement down to the right place.

Moving on a Pulley

3 1833 05143 6803

The workers are moving a bucket. They are using a pulley. Pulleys help move heavy things.

This machine is a crane. It is a big pulley. It moves big things.

Moving with Shovels and Scoops

Workers are moving dirt with a shovel. A shovel is a machine called a **lever**.

The **scoop** of a bulldozer is a lever, too. It helps move big **piles** of dirt.

Moving on Wheels

Axle

Many machines move on wheels. Each pair of wheels is on an **axle**.

A steamroller is a machine with a big, wide wheel. It makes dirt very flat.

Moving Up and Down

A well driller moves up and down. It pushes a giant drill bit into the ground.

A jackhammer moves much faster than a well driller.
It has a pointed end. It breaks things apart.

Moving People

A scissor lift holds people who are working on the building. Lifts move people up and down.

A cherry picker can move workers up and down, too. The arm of the cherry picker is a lever.

Moving a Machine

Some machines are used to move other machines. This dirt mover is being moved to a new job.

Big machines are needed to move other machines around the work site.

Try It!

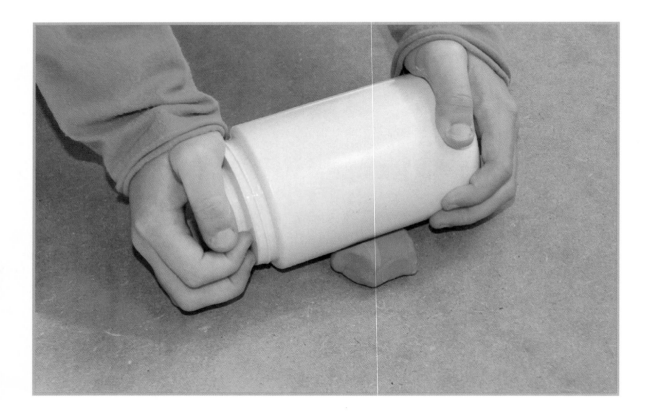

Make a steamroller with a can. Now you can make the clay very flat.

GLOSSARY

axle (AK suhl): long, thin pole with wheels on each end

construction site (kuhn STRUKT shun SITE): a place where workers build

lever (LEV ur): a simple machine used to lift things

machine (muh SHEEN): something that uses energy to help people work

pile (PILE): a heap or mound of something

scoop (SKOOP): the shovel part of a bulldozer or back hoe

wheelbarrow (WEEL ba roh): a bucket with wheels that workers can move

INDEX

FURTHER READING

Fowler, Allan. *Simple Machines.* Children's Press, New York: 2001
Kilby, Don. *At a Construction Site.* Kids Can Press, 2003.
Tocci, Salvatore. *Experiments with Simple Machines.*
    Children's Press, 2003.

WEBSITES TO VISIT

http://www.edheads.org/activities/simple-machines/index.htm
http://science.howstuffworks.com/engineering-channel.htm
http://www.bobthebuilder.com/usa/index.html

ABOUT THE AUTHOR

Patty Whitehouse has been a teacher for 17 years. She is currently a Lead Science teacher in Chicago, where she lives with her husband and two teenage children. She is the author of more than 100 books about science for children.